The Golden Ghost

The Golden Ghost

by *Marion Dane Bauer*

illustrated by *Peter Ferguson*

A STEPPING STONE BOOK™

Random House New York

To Polly and Daisy, my favorite dinner guests —M.D.B.

For Robbie and Hannah —P.F.

Text copyright © 2011 by Marion Dane Bauer
Illustrations copyright © 2011 by Peter Ferguson

Published in the United States by Random House Children's Books,
a division of Random House, Inc., New York.

Random House and the colophon are registered trademarks and A Stepping Stone
Book and the colophon are trademarks of Random House, Inc.

Visit us on the Web!
SteppingStonesBooks.com
www.randomhouse.com/kids

Educators and librarians, for a variety of teaching tools, visit us at
www.randomhouse.com/teachers

Library of Congress Cataloging-in-Publication Data
Bauer, Marion Dane.
The golden ghost / Marion Dane Bauer ; illustrated by Peter Ferguson. — 1st ed.
    p.   cm.
"A Stepping Stone book."
Summary: On a bike outing to the abandoned houses by the old cement mill,
Delsie and her friend Todd discover one of the houses is not empty—and a ghost
dog haunts the area.
ISBN 978-0-375-86649-4 (trade hardcover) — ISBN 978-0-375-96649-1 (lib. bdg.) —
ISBN 978-0-375-89818-1 (ebook)
[1. Dogs—Fiction. 2. Ghosts—Fiction. 3. Homeless persons—Fiction.] I. Ferguson,
Peter, ill. II. Title.
PZ7.B3262Go 2011 [Fic]—dc22 2010004116

Printed in the United States of America
10 9 8 7 6 5 4 3 2 1

Contents

Chapter 1
Ghost Houses

*T*he big dog was pacing, pacing. She moved in a steady loping trot around the small house. She made one circle with her nose to the ground. She made another testing the air.

From time to time she ran onto the front porch of the house and checked up there.

Then she went back to circling again.

She ran without pause. She seemed to run without effort, too. She didn't pant. She didn't slow her pace. The big dog just kept running.

Her silky reddish-gold fur rippled with each step. Her eyes were dark with knowing. She had been alone and lonely for so long. She had been waiting for so long.

When would someone see her?

At last, she stopped in front of the house. She sat, pointed her soft muzzle at the summer sky, and howled. The cry drifted out and out.

Away from the empty house.

Away from the empty cement mill that stood like a sentinel over the scene.

Into the empty blue sky.

The big dog cocked her head, waiting for some kind of reply.

When no response came, she went back to pacing.

Pacing.

Pacing.

* * *

Delsie and Todd sat on the curb in front of the grocery store.

Delsie scuffed her feet in the gravel that had gathered in the gutter. She scooped some into her hand and let it trickle between her fingers.

Panning for gold, she thought. *We could pan for gold.*

But when she looked over at Todd, she didn't say it.

He seemed to have run out of patience with her ideas. And maybe she had run out of good ideas, too.

Just as they had run out of summer.

Here it was Labor Day weekend. School started in three days. And they had nothing better to do than sit on the curb in front of her parents' grocery store.

Bug, Todd's small black and tan dog, lay at their feet, panting. Apparently, he didn't have any good ideas, either.

Delsie lifted the little dog onto her lap. "Why did they name you Bug?" she asked him. "You're too cute to be called Bug."

It was an old complaint. When Bug was a new pup, Delsie had wanted to call him Shadow. That was what he looked like, a glossy black shadow with sunlight peeking out. His reddish-brown paws, his reddish-brown muzzle, and his sweet reddish-brown eyebrows were the sunlight. Mostly, though, he was shadow.

"Because his eyes are buggy," Todd answered, though she'd been talking to Bug, not to him. "Anyway, Ryan named him." Ryan was one of Todd's brothers.

Todd had three older brothers. He had

everything, really. Three older brothers. A dog. Two cats. He even had hamsters that kept making new hamsters until Todd and his brothers had to go all over town begging people to adopt them.

Delsie didn't have any brothers or sisters. She didn't have any pets, either. She didn't even have a hamster. "No dogs," Delsie's dad said. "No cats. No hamsters. No guinea pigs. No bunny rabbits. No little white mice. No groundhogs. I'm allergic."

Delsie's dad liked making jokes, though Delsie didn't think that one was very funny.

She had never asked for a groundhog.

Delsie rubbed inside one of Bug's floppy ears. He leaned into her hand and groaned with pleasure.

Bug was an odd-looking dog. His long, fringed tail was elegant. His snub nose was comical. They seemed like ends that belonged on two different dogs.

"Maybe he should have been called Prince," she said. "Or Clown. Just about anything would have been better than Bug."

Behind them, Delsie's father emerged from the store with a broom.

"Waiting for a taxi?" he asked.

That was a joke, too. Milton was a very small town. It had one grocery store, one school, and one old cement mill on the edge of town. The mill had shut down before Delsie and Todd were born. There were two churches and two taverns, too. ("One tavern for each church," Delsie's dad always said.)

No taxis.

Todd laughed, but Delsie didn't. She just said, "We're bored. We need something to do. Something spectacular."

"You could sweep the walk," her dad offered, holding out the broom. "A clean walk is always spectacular."

Delsie usually liked helping out around her parents' store. But not today, with the sun shining so brightly and the summer almost gone.

She kissed the top of Bug's head and ignored the broom.

Todd jumped up and took it. He would have stood on his head for Delsie's dad if he'd asked him to. Todd's father had moved to another state and rarely called.

"I wish I could have a dog," Delsie said. She said it loudly enough for her father to hear as he headed back inside the store.

Her father didn't slow his stride as he said over his shoulder, "No dogs. No cats. No hamsters—"

Delsie interrupted. "I know. No ground-hogs, either. You're allergic."

"Right!" her father said. The bell over the door jangled as the door fell closed.

Todd began sweeping, though there wasn't much on the walk except more gravelly dust.

Delsie stayed where she was. She rubbed Bug's other ear, and he groaned some more. How she wished she could have a dog of her own! Any kind of dog would do. Even one named Bug!

Maybe she could get a dog without any fur, if there was such a thing. If a dog didn't have any fur, would it still make her father sneeze?

Delsie didn't much mind being an only child. She didn't have to put up with teasing, except for her dad's. She didn't have to share her bedroom. She didn't have to watch her birthday cake disappear before she'd had seconds. Todd had to do all those things.

But while being an only child was okay, being a dogless one wasn't.

There seemed to be hardly a moment in Delsie's life when she wasn't longing for a dog. She missed having one most when she was waiting to fall asleep at night.

That was when she pretended her dog was there, snuggled in close beside her. She even slept on the very edge of her bed to make sure her dog had enough room. (It would be a girl dog, she'd decided.)

Delsie gave Bug a hard squeeze. He said "*Ooomph,*" and squirmed away. The street was empty, but still she looped her hand through his leash to keep him close.

Billows of dust rose from Todd's sweeping. Delsie got up to move out of the way with Bug.

"Is that all you're going to do?" she asked. "Sweep my dad's walk?"

"Do you have a better idea?" Todd said.

That was the problem, though, and Todd knew it. She was out of ideas.

She scrambled through her brain for something. "We could check out the ghost houses," she said after a thorough search. She didn't know where that idea had come from. Had it been lurking in a dark corner?

Todd stopped sweeping. He studied her, his eyes narrowed. "Are you serious?" he asked.

She hadn't been. Not really. But the look on Todd's face made her suddenly determined.

"Yeah," she said. "I'm serious. Why not?"

She waited for him to tell her it was a dumb idea.

The truth was she knew it was dumb. Every kid in town had been told not to hang around the empty old houses by the mill.

But Todd surprised her. "Okay." He took one last swish at the walk and leaned the broom against the storefront. "The ghost houses it is," he said. "Let's go."

It had been her idea. What could Delsie do but follow?

Chapter 2

Through the Open Door

As Delsie pedaled behind Todd's bike toward the edge of town, she had plenty of time for regrets.

People were always telling her that she let her imagination run away with her. Even Todd said that sometimes, and he was her best friend. Here she'd gone and proven the point again. Who wanted to check out ghost houses, anyway?

They weren't really ghost houses, of course. That was just what the kids called them. They were houses that had been built for the long-ago workers at the cement mill.

Now they stood staring at one another across an empty street, as silent and dusty as the abandoned mill. No one lived in them now. No one had lived in them for a long time.

The kids in town liked to say that ghosts lived there . . . if what ghosts did could be called living. Boys were always daring one another to check them out.

Why hadn't she suggested going back to Todd's house instead? They could have run through the sprinkler. Or they could have made popcorn and watched one of Todd's mom's old movies.

What was wrong with imagining ordinary things like that?

Todd had pulled ahead. Delsie sighed and pumped harder. At least the mill wasn't very far.

They bumped across the rusty railroad tracks that led to the old mill. Beyond the tracks Todd stopped in the long grass beside the road. He stepped off his bike.

Delsie jumped off her bike next to him. She pulled off her helmet and wiped her sweaty cheek against her sleeve. Then she looked back at the old mill looming above them.

A smokestack rammed itself against the blue of the sky. There was a bank of silos, too, and some old buildings. All of it was the dirty white of old cement dust. All of it was silent and empty.

The houses were strung along a red-gravel street in the shadow of the mill.

They looked pretty much alike. They were square and small and as empty as the mill.

The street was deserted, too. Patches of scraggly grass sprouted here and there in the gravel.

Just standing in the middle of all that emptiness made Delsie's arms prickle into goose bumps.

She gave herself a shake.

What was the harm, anyway? The only thing they were doing was checking out a bunch of old houses. She might have a good imagination, but she didn't believe in ghosts.

At least she didn't think she did.

Still, she said, "It's not so hot anymore. Maybe we should just keep riding instead."

It was true that the day seemed cooler now. In fact, here, beneath the mill, an odd chill touched the air.

Todd gave her arm a poke. "Aw, come on," he said. "It was your idea. You're not going to chicken out, are you?"

Delsie thought of turning the moment into a joke. All she'd have to do was flap her elbows and squawk like a chicken. What stopped her was the thing Todd always said about her. That she wasn't like *other* girls.

By that he meant she wasn't prissy, worried about getting her clothes dirty . . . scared.

So she said instead, "Of course I'm not chicken." Then she added, "Which one should we check out first?"

"That one." Todd nodded in the direction of the nearest house.

They dropped their bikes in the grass, and Todd moved out ahead of her. He jumped up the steps onto a rickety porch. He reached for the doorknob.

It rattled in his hand, but the door didn't open.

"Shoot!" Todd said.

Delsie was careful not to let her relief show. If all the houses were locked, they couldn't go in, could they?

She stepped up onto the porch and

pressed her nose against the front window. It was so dark inside she couldn't make out much.

What had she expected? Ghosts didn't need to turn on lights to see.

The house next door was locked, too. The front windows on this one had been broken and were boarded up, so they went around to the side.

They peered through a small window into what seemed to be a bathroom.

Would ghosts need a bathroom? Delsie wondered.

"You see that ghost on the toilet?" Todd asked, as if he could read her mind. Actually, sometimes she thought he *could* read her mind.

"No, only the werewolf in the bathtub," she said.

He gave her arm a poke again, a little harder than he needed to.

Delsie rubbed the spot, but she didn't say anything.

The next house was locked . . . and the next and the next.

This wasn't so bad. Two more houses and they would be at the end of the street. After that they could cross over and do the other side, stare into the windows, stare into the empty dark. Then they could go home.

What was so scary about that?

When they were back at school on Tuesday, they could brag about checking out the ghost houses. The boys would be impressed. Some of the girls probably would be, too.

The prissy girls would say it was a dumb thing to do. But they would be impressed anyway.

Delsie ran ahead of Todd to the next house. She bounded up onto the porch and reached for the doorknob. Two people could play this game! She'd rattle the locked door, and then she'd say, "Shoot!"

The doorknob felt smooth in her hand. The metal was cool. And it turned easily.

It turned and the door swung open.

Delsie sucked in her breath.

She looked at Todd. His face had gone pale beneath his sandy hair and his scattering of summer freckles.

"Well," he said. Then he didn't say anything more.

She waited.

"I guess this is it," he said finally. "Come on."

And he stepped ahead of her through the open door.

Chapter 3
Goldilocks

*D*elsie stood on the porch for a long moment, waiting for Todd to come back. Who did he think he was, anyway—Goldilocks? You didn't just barge into a stranger's house like that.

She glanced over her shoulder at the mill. Then she looked up and down the street.

Why was this house unlocked?

What—or who—was waiting inside?

Not a ghost, surely. Ghosts wouldn't need to unlock doors. At least the ghosts you read about in stories wouldn't.

Finally, standing on the empty porch on the empty street by herself grew more scary than being inside with Todd. So Delsie stepped through the doorway, too.

The house was . . . well, it was just a house. There was even a bit of furniture.

Nothing fancy, that was for sure. A sagging couch stood along one wall. It looked like a leftover from a garage sale. The "coffee table" in front of the couch was a piece of plywood with cement blocks for legs. Stuffing poked out of the arms of a big blue easy chair.

There was a small television set, the kind with rabbit ears on top. Delsie didn't think those even worked anymore.

But then maybe ghosts didn't need antennae to watch TV.

She shuddered. She had to stop all this ghost stuff.

And where was Todd, anyway?

Just as she asked herself the question, he appeared in the doorway of one of the side rooms, probably a bedroom.

"It's almost like somebody really lives here," she whispered. She hadn't meant to whisper. It was the way her words came out.

"Yeah," Todd said. He was whispering, too.

He didn't pause, though. He moved on to the next room. Delsie followed. This was the kitchen. And if the first room had seemed odd, the kitchen was even stranger.

There was a single chair and a rickety table. The table was set. It was actually set with a spoon and a bowl and a mug. The mug looked as though it had once had coffee in it. Brown sludge lined the bottom.

The bowl was crusty. Old oatmeal? Did ghosts eat oatmeal?

But she was being silly.

This wasn't a ghost house. A real person lived here. And that was probably worse.

They had walked into a real person's house. If they got caught, whoever lived here wasn't going to be thinking about Goldilocks. He was going to be thinking about calling the police!

The same thought must have come to Todd at the same instant, because he said, "Come on," exactly the way he had earlier. Only this time he was heading out the door.

Delsie followed.

At least she started to follow, but after a step or two, something stopped her. She had no idea what it was. Whatever it was bumped softly against her leg, held her in place.

It might have been Bug. It seemed as silky and soft as Bug. She automatically looked down so she wouldn't step on the little dog. How had he gotten here? Hadn't they left him behind in Todd's yard with the gate bolted?

But what she saw wasn't Bug. It was . . . nothing.

Whatever had brushed against her had been much larger than Bug, anyway. It had reached nearly to the top of her thigh.

She looked around again. Again she saw nothing except a plain linoleum floor, old and stained and dirty. There was the chair and the table with the crusty bowl and the spoon and the mug. There was the sludge of leftover coffee in the bottom of the mug.

Delsie reached down and around her on every side, feeling for whatever had stopped her.

Nothing.

And yet she could have sworn that something had bumped into her.

"Come on, Delsie," Todd called from the porch. "Are you nuts? Somebody lives here. Breaking and entering. That's what they call it when you go into somebody's house without permission."

Delsie started for the door.

After a few steps, she stopped again. She knew Todd was right. They didn't belong in here. But . . .

But what?

She didn't know, except that it had been something. Something silky and just about thigh-high had bumped into her.

She looked around at the sagging couch, the plywood table, the out-of-date TV. Then she gave herself a shake and ran out the door.

Todd waited on the cracked sidewalk. He didn't say anything when she reached him. He just started jogging toward their bikes.

She followed.

Delsie kept looking back, though. She couldn't help it.

The big dog followed the children along the empty street.

Her owner had gone off again. Sometimes she followed him when he left. Sometimes she didn't. It didn't seem to make much difference either way. He never saw her any longer.

These children, though, were a different story. Especially the girl. The golden dog was almost certain the girl had seen her. Or at least she had come close to seeing her.

That seeing—that near seeing—drew the big dog like a magnet.

When the children rode off in the same direction her owner had gone earlier, she paused for a moment, considering. If she followed, if she at least went a short distance in that direction, she might find him.

Her owner.

Or the girl.

Either one would do.

Her plumed tail lifting, the golden dog set off after the bikes.

Chapter 4

The Last Sips of Summer

*D*inner at Delsie's house was chicken salad. It was chicken salad with raisins in it. Delsie liked chicken salad well enough, but she hated raisins.

When she was a little kid, she'd tried to throw away a whole carton of raisins from the grocery storeroom. Her plan had been to haul them to the woods behind the store and hide them. She'd figured that if the store ran out of raisins, her mother would have to quit putting them into everything.

Her dad had caught her halfway across the backyard, tugging on the heavy box. He'd thought it was funny. He'd called her the raisin thief.

Even now, when he looked at the pile of raisins on the edge of her plate, he said, "So what kind of a day has our raisin thief had?" His voice came out brightly cheerful, the way it always did when he tried to be funny.

"Fine," Delsie said. She extracted another raisin. Then, before he could ask her something else, she asked, "Does anybody still live in the ghost hou— I mean, the old mill houses?"

Her mother frowned. "Nobody's lived there for years," she said. "Not since the mill shut down."

"Why?" her father asked. He was suddenly serious, too. "You and Todd haven't been poking around there, have you?"

"Oh . . . we just rode our bikes near there," Delsie said. "And I got to wondering. That's all." She concentrated on another raisin that had attached itself to a piece of celery.

It wasn't quite a lie.

"Well, you know you're not—" her father started to say.

But just then the bell on the door downstairs jangled. That meant a customer had come into the store. Instead of finishing his sentence, Delsie's father pushed his chair back from the table.

It was probably Miss Daley.

Most people avoided coming into the store during suppertime. They knew the family would be upstairs eating. But Miss Daley wasn't most people. She seemed to pick suppertime nearly every day to run out of milk. Or she suddenly needed tea bags or a box of crackers, some little thing like that.

When Dad came back from waiting on her, he always reported on what she had bought.

Mom said Miss Daley came in then because she knew she could have Dad to herself . . . no other customers. No Mom, either.

Dad just laughed when Mom said that.

"Here's our daily customer," he said now. And he chuckled at his own joke even though he made it every time.

After he'd gone, Delsie began counting her raisins. She had gotten to twelve when her mother started in where her father had left off. "Delsie," she said, "you and Todd aren't—"

"No, of course not!" Delsie exclaimed. And to her relief, that was the end of the conversation.

When Delsie's dad came back, her mom asked, "Was it Miss Daley?"

"No," he replied. "It was an old man. I've

seen him once or twice before, but I don't know who he is."

Someone her dad didn't know? Delsie was surprised. He usually knew everyone who came into the store.

"Bob Holtz told me he thought some old guy was camping out in one of the mill houses," her dad added. "Homeless, I guess. Maybe he's the one."

A homeless man camping out in one of the mill houses! Delsie pushed away from the table. She hurried to the windows at the front of the living room so she could look out at the street.

There he was, heading in the direction of the mill. The man had a thin ponytail of white hair hanging down his back. He wore overalls and, despite the heat, a long-sleeved flannel shirt.

Was he the one? Was it his house she and Todd had been in?

And what was that following him? She couldn't quite make it out.

It could have been a collection of fireflies, glimmering in the evening light.

It could have been . . . nothing.

Just her imagination again.

Still, she wanted a closer look. So she called, trying to sound casual, "I'm finished with supper. I think I'll go out and ride my bike for a little while."

"Trying to get in your last sips of summer?" her mother replied. She said it in the kind of understanding mother-voice that made Delsie feel instantly guilty.

What would her mom say if she knew Delsie was going out to follow a stranger?

But it wasn't the stranger . . . it was the glimmer in the air right behind him. It was the unforgettable feeling of something silky brushing against her thigh.

Somehow—Delsie didn't know quite how—the two were connected. She was certain of it.

Delsie hurried down the stairs.

Chapter 5

Ghost Dog!

$\mathcal{D}$elsie pedaled hard along the quiet street. The man wasn't far ahead of her on the sidewalk. She passed him quickly.

He had a grocery bag in each hand. The small plastic kind. They didn't look heavy, but he walked as though they weighed him down. He walked as though *something* weighed him down. He didn't even look up as she rode by.

What was it like to be homeless?

What was it like to be homeless and to be followed around by a collection of fireflies? That was what it had looked like when she'd seen him from their apartment. It was what it looked like still.

Was there some kind of shape in the glimmering?

Or was the whole thing her imagination? Todd called it her "girly" imagination when he was annoyed with her. Sometimes it seemed that "girly" was the worst word he knew.

Delsie made a U-turn and pedaled back. She stopped her bike before she reached the man and waited for him to approach.

A car swooshed by, turned the corner, and disappeared. There weren't many cars on the street in Milton in the evening.

"Hi," she said when the man reached her.

His head jerked up. Hadn't he known she was there? For a fraction of a second, he hesitated. But then his head dropped again, and he walked on by.

He hadn't even said hi. Nobody in Milton ever walked past without saying hi.

Delsie shrugged and climbed back onto her bike.

But before she could resume pedaling, there it was again . . . the glimmer. And this time, she could make out a golden shape.

The shape followed at the man's heels as though it were . . . almost as though it were . . .

A dog?

Could it be? A large golden dog?

And then . . . suddenly . . . she could see it clearly. See it, but see through it at the same time.

Square head. Floppy ears. The silken fur rippled with each step. The dark eyes looked at her, looked right inside her.

I want you, the eyes said. *And I know you want me.*

Delsie held out a hand in invitation. The dog hesitated. She stretched her neck to sniff Delsie's hand. But then she turned her head away . . . sadly, Delsie thought.

The dog stayed close behind the man.

Was she real? How could she be? She was a dog that seemed to be made up of a million tiny lights.

Or was she a ghost?

Who ever heard of a ghost dog?

Who ever heard of a ghost *anything* outside of stories?

But there she was, walking along in a sparkling dog shape.

Delsie stared after the magnificent creature. Her great tail waved slowly from side to side. She stayed so close behind the old man, she might have been leashed. But there was no leash.

Anyway, no laws said *ghost* dogs had to be leashed. Did they?

Delsie didn't know how she felt about the idea of a ghost dog. She didn't know how she should feel. She had never believed in ghosts particularly. No more than any other kid when stories were being told around a campfire on a dark night.

But it wasn't even night yet. The sun still rode halfway down the sky.

It was early evening, a perfectly ordinary evening in Milton. Except for a ghost dog walking down Main Street.

If Todd saw the dog, if *only* Todd saw the dog, he wouldn't be able to complain about her imagination ever again. Not in a million, trillion years!

Delsie drew in her breath. Then she turned her bike around and headed for

Todd's house, passing the old man and the golden dog once more. Todd's house lay about two blocks ahead. If she hurried, she could get him outside in time to see the ghost dog.

She dropped her bike in front of Todd's house and took the steps to the porch in a single bound. She knocked and rang the doorbell at the same time.

Bug responded with a flurry of barks.

Then when Todd opened the door, Bug flew through it. Delsie had prepared herself for the onslaught. Bug always threw himself at her, scrabbling at her legs as though he meant to climb her. But this time he had other ideas. He barreled right past. He flung himself off the porch and across the front yard, yapping.

Bug ran at the man and the golden dog,

making a noise that would have done credit to ten little dogs.

"Bug!" Todd yelled after him. He turned to Delsie and added in the same cross voice, "What's wrong with him, anyway?" He said it as though *she* had caused Bug to lose his little doggy mind.

"Bug!" he yelled again. And he leapt off the front porch, too.

But Bug was paying no attention to
Todd. Instead, he was dancing and barking.
Barking and dancing.

He paid no attention to the man, either.
He danced around the glimmering golden
dog, barking his head off.

The big dog stood patiently. She glowed patiently. She might have been waiting for Bug to learn some manners.

"Bug!" Delsie called. "Don't!"

The man had stopped in the middle of the sidewalk. "Dad-blasted dog!" he yelled. "Get away from me!"

And he swung at Bug. First he swung one of his bags of groceries. The bag missed.

Then he swung a booted foot.

The foot connected.

Bug yelped, a single piercing cry. He turned and barreled back toward the house. His ears flowed out behind him. He held his long, plumed tail tight beneath his belly.

Delsie couldn't believe that anyone— anyone in the world—could kick a dog. Especially sweet little Bug!

"You!" she yelled at the old man. She ran

at him. "How could you? He wasn't doing anything to you!"

"He was jumping at me," the man said. He swiped his nose with the back of a grimy hand, still holding one of the bags of groceries. "He had his mouth open, and he was jumping at me."

"He wasn't jumping at *you*!" Delsie protested. "He was jumping at your—"

But Todd interrupted. "You didn't have to kick him!" he yelled. "Bug's never bitten anybody in his life!"

Todd didn't stay to finish the argument, though. He followed Bug back to the house and sat on the porch steps, gathering his little dog into his arms. Delsie was left alone to face the man.

The man fixed his gaze on Delsie. "I hate dogs!" he growled. His bushy white eyebrows were knotted fiercely. "I hate every single one of them."

Even as the man spoke, the golden dog gazed lovingly into his face. He might have been saying wonderful things . . . to her, about her.

How could she be following such a cruel master, anyway?

Delsie stepped toward the man. "We know where you're staying," she said in a low, threatening voice. "You're camping out in one of the mill houses, and we know it."

He didn't say anything, but his face pinched together as if he'd been slapped.

"That's breaking and entering, you know," Delsie went on. "We'll tell the police, and they'll put you in jail. That's where you belong! Jail!"

Delsie didn't know whether the police

cared that the man was staying in one of the mill houses, but they ought to. They ought to care about anybody who kicked a little dog.

The man poked out his chin. "They won't need to bother looking," he said. "Because I won't be there. I'll be gone before they get a chance."

And he turned and started up the street again. Incredibly, the golden dog still followed him.

If only Todd could see . . .

But Delsie hadn't even tried to show him.

"Todd!" she called. "Todd . . . look!" She pointed at the retreating figure.

Todd sat with his arms wrapped around Bug. The little dog waggled from head to toe, licking Todd's face. Obviously he had recovered from the kick.

"What?" Todd asked. But he was folded over Bug and didn't look up.

"It's . . ." Delsie pointed harder after the retreating man and the collection of golden sparkles. "It's . . . ," she tried again.

Then she let her hand drop.

"Never mind," she said.

The pair was too far away already. She could hardly make out the dog shape herself, and she knew how to look. All she could see now were a few sparkles.

Todd would never see the golden dog from this distance.

What would she tell him to look for, anyway? Something that looked like a gathering of fireflies? Something that was supposed to be a dog but that you could see right through?

Besides, maybe a person had to *want* to

see the golden dog to be able to see her. Maybe a person of great imagination had to want very much to see her.

Delsie turned back toward Todd and Bug—Todd's very solid little dog.

Chapter 6

Moving On!

The golden dog followed the man, but she kept turning her head to watch the girl. She watched and watched.

She loved the man. She had loved him since they had found one another when she was barely more than a pup. That had been a cold night in a much larger city. She had been young and homeless and hungry. He was homeless and hungry, too, though not so young.

They had kept one another warm that first night. And from then on, they had stayed together.

They shared all that came to them. Often it wasn't much. Food the old man found in Dumpsters behind restaurants and bakeries. An occasional rabbit the golden dog caught. Maybe a shed far enough away from a farmhouse to be safe for shelter. Or a large cardboard box behind some bushes in a park.

Sometimes the man had work. When that happened, he brought food from a grocery store. But soon—the golden dog never knew why—they would be moving again. And then they would be hungry again. Both of them hungry.

The day came when the dog began to grow sick. She didn't know she was sick. She knew only that the rabbits seemed to run faster. She knew that even the food the man put down in front of her wasn't appealing.

The two of them stayed close still. Wherever they slept, they slept side by side. The man with his arm thrown across her deep chest. The man with his rough fingers tangled in her golden fur.

The dog slept more and more, and the man stayed close. He stayed close until hunger and cold slipped away . . . for the dog, anyway.

The golden dog barely noticed the slipping. She simply lay beneath the welcome weight of the man's arm and breathed and breathed . . . until she breathed no more.

When her breath was gone, she stayed on. The man was the only human who had ever needed her, so she stayed.

He didn't speak to her. He clearly no longer knew she was there. But the very rage with which he tackled the world told her how much he needed her still.

And so she stayed close.

Staying didn't keep her from being lonely,
though. If anything, being close to the unseeing
man made her longing deeper.

Until the girl. The girl had seen. The girl had
seen, and she wanted her.

But how could she leave the man?

The golden dog plodded down the street,
following.

Delsie sat down on the porch and put a hand
on Bug's round little head.

"Are you okay?" she asked.

Bug leapt up and licked her chin.

"I guess he's okay," she said to Todd.

Todd nodded, but he kept stroking Bug
from head to tail, checking for injury.

"Do you know what he was barking at?"
Delsie asked.

"The old man," he answered. "What else?"

Delsie took a deep breath. She knew it was useless to tell him. But because it was Todd and because they had always told one another everything, she kept going.

"He was barking at the old man's dog," she said. "It's a ghost dog, really. More a collection of sparkles than anything."

Todd didn't reply.

Delsie put a hand beneath Bug's chin and tipped his head up. She gazed into his solemn brown eyes. Bug had seen the golden dog. She knew for certain that he had.

She waited to see what Todd would say.

"Do you know what?" Todd said finally.

"What?" she asked. She kept her gaze on Bug's large, round eyes.

"Sometimes I think you're nuts," Todd said. "Positively nuts."

Delsie winced. But if Todd had just told her he'd seen a ghost dog and she hadn't seen the same thing, wasn't that what she would have said?

Maybe.

Maybe not.

"I think I'll go home," she said. And she stood.

"What do you want to do tomorrow?" Todd called after her when she was halfway down the walk.

"I don't know," she answered, not looking

back. "Probably nothing. Nothing at all."

Maybe they were getting too old to be best friends. Her mother had told her that might happen. She said that someday they might feel too old to be best friends, a boy and a girl. She'd said things would happen that would make everything different.

Delsie didn't think her mom had been talking about ghosts, though.

Still, Delsie was angry. She hadn't said it. She hadn't even let her voice sound like it. But she was good and angry.

Why couldn't Todd let himself see what was right in front of his eyes? Was it just because she was a girl? Because he was a boy and what he saw was always bigger, more important, than anything she might see?

She headed for her apartment above the store.

* * *

As the man approached the row of houses, he walked faster. He swung the two bags with their scant groceries.

Blasted kids! What were they doing interfering? He wasn't hurting anybody, staying in that little house. Why should a house be sitting there empty when there were people like him in the world who didn't have a roof? Didn't have anything.

Not that it mattered. There wasn't much that seemed to matter now that Dog was gone.

It was time to move on. The cold would be coming soon, and there would be no way to get heat in that abandoned little house. He was running out of odd jobs in this hick town, anyway.

Still . . . he hated being told. Always had. It was almost like having the police say it. "Move on! Move on!" That annoying kid and her "We'll tell the police."

That infernal little black dog, barking at his heels.

He hadn't been able to stand the sight of a dog, any dog, since Dog had died.

His dog.

No name. He'd never given her a name.

He felt bad about that sometimes. She'd deserved a name.

Sometimes he almost thought he saw her again . . . hanging around, right close by. Just a glimpse of that golden fur. Those eyes.

But he wasn't crazy. He wasn't like those guys who got hauled away every now and then. Seeing stuff. Yelling about what they were seeing.

He knew what was what.

Dog was dead. That was all. Dead meant gone. He'd buried her himself behind the little house. Dug a hole deep so no wild animal would come out of the woods and dig her up.

Dug a hole and that was the end of it.

Except now he'd have to go off and leave her here. There was nothing to be done about that.

As the man walked up the steps to the porch, though, the nothing he could do was suddenly too much. He kicked the face of a step. Kicked hard, meaning it to hurt. Hurt his foot. Hurt the step.

He intended to make a solid thump.

He'd spent years—he no longer knew how many—without a home, and he'd never made any noise. Sneaking around. Hiding in boxes, in sheds, in abandoned houses no one had bothered to tear down.

If anyone had known he wanted to live in this one, they probably would have torn it down. They would have hauled it away before he got a chance.

But the thump his foot made wasn't solid. When he kicked, his foot passed right through the front of the half-rotten step. His foot passed through and his ankle caught.

And then he was falling backward . . . falling.

Chapter 7

Home

$\mathcal{D}$elsie was halfway home when a soft touch on her hand startled her. It was a damp, cool touch.

She looked down and, at first, saw nothing.

Then the golden dog gathered before her eyes. The dog trotted along beside Delsie, her cool nose grazing Delsie's palm.

Come, the cool nose said. And the liquid brown eyes said, *Come.*

Delsie stopped walking.

Again, a nudge from the nose.

"What's wrong?" Delsie asked.

But the dog only turned away. Then she looked back over her shoulder to see if Delsie was following.

Delsie's first thought was that something had happened to Todd.

But when she neared Todd's house, she could see that he still sat on the front steps, Bug cradled in his arms.

Bug leapt down and ran toward Delsie. Or rather he ran at the golden dog. He danced around both of them, barking grandly.

The golden dog looked down from her much greater height and kept right on walking. When Delsie stopped, the big dog paused a short distance away and looked back. She was clearly still expecting Delsie to follow.

Delsie scooped Bug into her arms and ran toward the porch. "Put him away," she told Todd. "Put him away and come with me."

She didn't mean it to be a test, but the moment she said it, she knew it was. Would Todd trust her? Would he come when she asked just because they were friends?

She saw him hesitate. She saw the question rising in his eyes. And then she saw him decide.

He plucked Bug from her arms, put him inside the house, and asked, "Where are we going?"

It was a good thing they had decided to take Todd's bike. Delsie's was at home, so she'd ridden sidesaddle on his crossbar. They'd reached the abandoned little house much faster that way.

And once they got there and saw the old man lying at the base of the steps, Todd could go quickly for help. The man wasn't dead. He was still breathing, but he was quiet . . . very quiet. It was almost as if he'd gone to sleep in the middle of the sidewalk.

Todd had ridden to the first occupied house at the edge of town and asked them to call 911.

Now Delsie and Todd stood side by side and watched the ambulance pull away.

"How did you know?" Todd asked. "What made you come back here?"

Delsie looked over at the golden dog. She sat in the middle of the grass-pocked street, gazing after the ambulance as it turned the corner.

Delsie shrugged. "You'd never believe me," she said.

Todd gave her a long, hard look. "Try me," he said.

And so she explained . . . or tried to.

She could tell about the silken softness, the slight pressure that had held her in place when they were inside the house that first time.

She could talk about golden sparkles. She could say that the sparkles had taken the shape of a dog.

She could even tell about the cool nose in the palm of her hand. And she could describe the way the dark eyes had said, *Come.*

But she couldn't make Todd *see* what stood right in front of him. The golden ghost.

"She's beautiful," Delsie said finally. There seemed nothing more to say.

"How do you know it's a girl?" he asked.

"I just looked at her face, and I could tell," Delsie said.

Todd gave a little snort. "That's not the usual end you check," he said.

She shrugged. Some things never changed. Boys had to be funny.

The great dog rose from her place in the empty street and moved toward the porch. She brushed by so close that Delsie reached out and let a hand flow down her silken back.

Todd blinked, but he didn't move. Had he felt something?

"Here, girl," Delsie called softly. "Come on, girl. He's gone to the hospital. You can come with me now."

But the dog kept moving away.

Todd stared in the direction the dog had gone. Then he turned to study Delsie. "Your dad wouldn't be allergic to a ghost dog," he said.

Delsie laughed.

After a moment she asked, "Do you think he'll be all right?"

"The old man?" Todd said.

"Yeah."

"The paramedics said they thought he'd be okay," Todd said. "They said he'd knocked himself out, falling. They'll take care of him in the hospital."

Delsie turned back to the dog. She sat at the base of the porch steps now, watching the house, watching them.

"Come on, girl," Delsie said. "Please, come."

The golden dog gazed at Delsie. She

actually looked as though she might want to come. But then she looked back over her shoulder at the house again and didn't move.

"Call her by her name," Todd whispered. "If you said her name, maybe she would come."

Delsie turned and gaped at him. He was looking toward the porch, but again Delsie couldn't tell what he might be seeing. He wasn't making fun of her, though. That much was clear.

"I . . . I don't know her name," she said. Then she added, "Besides, I think she means to stay. I think she loved that old man and she's going to wait for him here."

"But he won't be back," Todd said.

"No," she agreed. "He won't. Even when he gets better, they won't let him."

She and Todd stood there, side by side,

for several moments more. The blaze of sunset had dissolved, and the blue had leached out of the sky.

"Can you . . . ?" Delsie said finally.

"Can I see what you see?" Todd finished the question for her.

She nodded.

"No," he said. "I wish I could." And then he put a hand very gently on her arm and added in a big-brotherly way, "I think we'd better go home. Maybe we can come back sometimes . . . to see her, you know? Or at least *you* can see her."

Delsie nodded again.

Together they climbed onto his bike. She settled back into her friend's arms, and they started up the street. The front wheel wobbled for a few yards from the extra weight, but soon Todd got the bike under control.

Delsie looked back over Todd's shoulder toward the little house and the dog. She could see nothing . . . only the barest suggestion of a sparkle.

"I'll never have a dog," she said when they stopped in front of Todd's house.

The front door opened, and Bug flew out to greet them.

"I know," Todd said. "Because of your dad." He knelt in the grass to receive Bug and buried his face in the shining black fur. "There might be worse things, though," he added, his face still buried. "Worse than not having a dog."

Delsie looked down at her friend. His neck looked skinny . . . and sad, somehow. "I guess you're right," she said.

She wanted to give Todd a hug, but she didn't. She gave him a punch on the shoulder instead. Just hard enough to feel, but not hard enough to hurt.

Chapter 8
Sunshine

The golden dog was pacing, pacing. Around and around the little house.

The man was gone. She loved the man.

The girl was gone, too. The girl who saw her.

The dog circled and circled the little house.

She stopped at last and pointed her soft muzzle at the starry sky. "Arooooo," she called. "Arooooo!"

No one answered.

*She circled again . . . and again . . . and
again.*

*At last she stopped beneath the tree where the
boy and girl had stood. She snuffled through the
grass. She pushed her nose deep into the grass to
capture every fragment of smell.*

*She walked a few paces away from the tree,
away from the house. Then she sniffed again.*

She walked some more.

*By the time she reached the end of the street,
she was running. But not in circles. She ran in a
straight, true line.*

"Arooooo!" she called. "Arooooo!"

Delsie woke slowly. Had she heard something outside? Someone calling?

That wasn't possible. No one in Milton
was up at this time of night. Whatever
time it might be, no one was up and about.

Not even the town's two police officers.

Delsie turned onto her side and adjusted her sheet and the light blanket. It was cooler tonight. Summer was nearly over.

Only two more days were left before fourth grade.

Todd's whole family—well, Todd and his mother and his three brothers—were coming for a picnic on Monday.

Delsie would help Mom make deviled eggs. Delsie always put pecan bits in the mashed-up yolks. Deviled eggs with pecans were her dad's favorite. If they didn't watch him, he would eat them all before anyone else had a chance. At least he'd say he'd eat them if he wasn't watched.

She turned again so she faced the door. Even as she turned, she scooted over to leave room on the bed. The way she always did.

She closed her eyes, but almost immediately they popped open again.

What was that? That glimmer. Had a lightning bug gotten in? A dozen lightning bugs? More?

And then there it was again. Right next to her bed this time. Not just a light. Not even a collection of lights. But a shape. A dog.

"Hello, Sunshine," Delsie whispered. She didn't know where the name had come from, but she knew it was right. She reached out a hand, then pulled it back. She didn't want to scare her dog.

But Sunshine wasn't scared. She climbed into the space that waited for her. The space that had been waiting for her for so long.

The ghost dog stretched herself out along the length of Delsie's body with a slight *"oooomph."* Then she laid her great head on Delsie's arm.

Her head was as light as feathers, but still Delsie could feel the weight of it, like a presence in a dream. Her fur was as silky-soft as Delsie had known it would be.

Delsie laid her other arm across Sunshine's chest and tangled her fingers in the golden fur.

"You're here," she breathed. "At last!"

Sunshine made a sound, deep in her throat, a comforting rumble almost like a purr.

Delsie was pretty sure that it meant "At last!" too.

About the Author

Marion Dane Bauer is the author of more than seventy books for children, including the Newbery Honor–winning *On My Honor*. She has also won the Kerlan Award for her collected work. Marion's first Stepping Stone book, *The Blue Ghost,* was named to the Texas Bluebonnet Award Master List. Marion has recently retired from the faculty of the Vermont College Master of Fine Arts in Writing for Children and Young Adults program.

Marion has nine grandchildren and lives in St. Paul, Minnesota.

About the Illustrator

Peter Ferguson has illustrated such books
as the Sisters Grimm series, the Lucy Rose
series, and *The Anybodies* and its sequels, and
he has painted the covers for many others.
He lives in Montreal with his wife, Eriko,
and cat, Yoda.